The front cover

Where is Chloe the chameleon?

Where do you think chameleons live?

What do you notice about her tongue? Why is it shaped like this?

What do you think chameleons eat?

The back cover

Read the blurb together.

How do you think chameleons catch flies for food?

The title page

What do you notice about the words 'Chloe' and 'chameleon'? (*they both start with 'ch'*)

What sound does 'ch' normally make? Can you think of any 'ch' words? (*cheek, change, chore*)

What sound does 'ch' make in 'Chloe' and 'chameleon' (*'k'*)

Can you think of any more 'ch' words that make a 'k' sound? (*character, chemist, chorus*)

1

READ

Read pages 2 and 3

Purpose: To find out how Chloe could catch flies.

PAUSE

Pause at page 3

Where is Chloe sitting? Why is she red?

Which words rhyme on these pages? (*flick, lick, quick*)

READ

Read pages 4 and 5

Purpose: To find out where Chloe went and what colour she turned.

PAUSE

Pause at page 5

Why did Chloe go on to the orange flower?

What punctuation mark is at the end of 'A flick – a lick – but the fly was too quick!'? Why is it there? How should we read it?

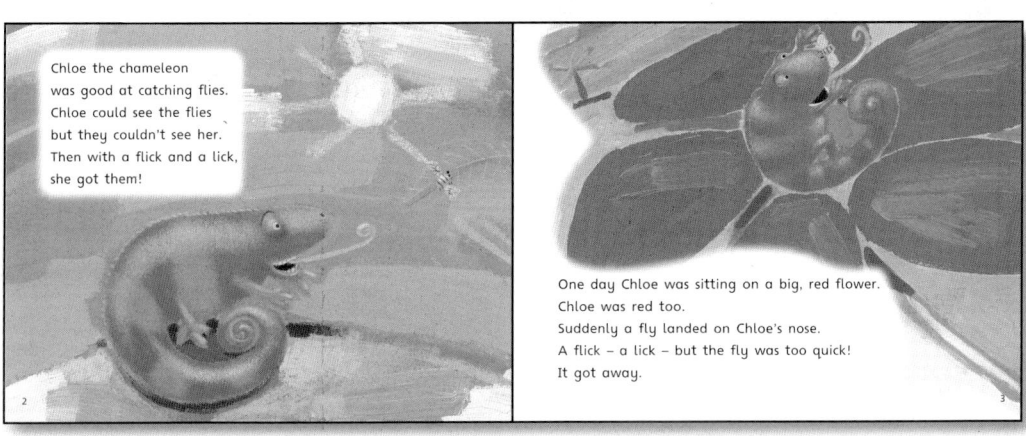

Chloe the chameleon was good at catching flies. Chloe could see the flies but they couldn't see her. Then with a flick and a lick, she got them!

One day Chloe was sitting on a big, red flower.
Chloe was red too.
Suddenly a fly landed on Chloe's nose.
A flick – a lick – but the fly was too quick!
It got away.

The fly went on to an orange flower.
Chloe went after the fly.
Soon Chloe was orange too.

Then the fly landed on Chloe's nose.
A flick – a lick – but the fly was too quick!
It got away.

Read pages 6 and 7

Purpose: To find out why Chloe turned yellow.

Pause at page 7

How does Chloe try to catch the fly? Why can't she manage to eat it?

Look at the words 'followed' and 'landed'. What do you notice about the endings? What does an 'ed' ending usually mean? (*Past tense, something that has already happened.*)

The fly went on to some yellow sand.
Chloe followed the fly and
soon Chloe was yellow too.

Then the fly landed on Chloe's nose.
A flick – a lick – but the fly was too quick!
It got away.

READ

Read pages 8 and 9

Purpose: To find out where Chloe went next and what colour she turned.

PAUSE

Pause at page 9

How does Chloe feel? How can you tell?

Can you see any 'ed' words on these pages?

The fly landed on a green leaf.
Chloe climbed the tree and
soon Chloe was as green as the leaf.

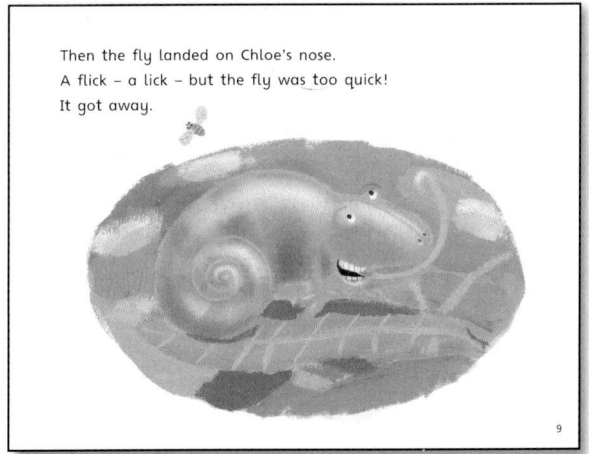

Then the fly landed on Chloe's nose.
A flick – a lick – but the fly was too quick!
It got away.

Read pages 10 and 11

Purpose: To find out where the fly went next and what colour Chloe turned.

Pause at page 11

Is Chloe enjoying herself? How do you know?

Who can read the sentence with all the rhyming words? Remember to read with expression.

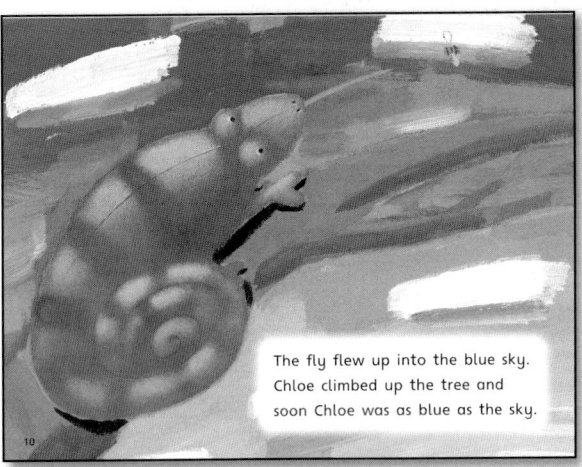

The fly flew up into the blue sky. Chloe climbed up the tree and soon Chloe was as blue as the sky.

Chloe saw the fly
but the fly didn't see Chloe.
A flick – a lick – but the fly was too quick!
It got away.

Read pages 12 and 13

Purpose: Find out what colour Chloe turned and why.

Pause at page 13

What is happening to the sky? (*The sky got darker.*)
What could this mean? (*nightfall or an impending rainstorm*)

What colour is indigo? Can anyone guess, using the context of the story? (Use a dictionary if necessary to aid vocabulary extension.)

The fly flew up into the sky.
Chloe climbed up the tree.
The sky got darker.
Soon the sky was indigo.
Chloe was indigo too.

Chloe saw the fly
but the fly didn't see Chloe.
A flick – a lick – but the fly was too quick!
It got away.

Read to the end

Purpose: To find out what happened to the fly and what happened to Chloe.

Pause at page 16

What do you notice about the sentence with the rhyming words? (Compare to the previous page).
This time Chloe was quick, not the fly.

On page 15 why is 'down, down, down' written as it is? What is the author trying to make us think?

Is this a happy ending? What makes you think this?

What do you notice after the word 'fly'? There's an ellipsis. Why is this? (*Because the tale could continue by going back to the start.*)

The sky got darker and darker.
Soon it was violet and
Chloe was violet too.
Then it began to rain.

With a flick and a lick – Chloe was quick!
This time she got the fly!

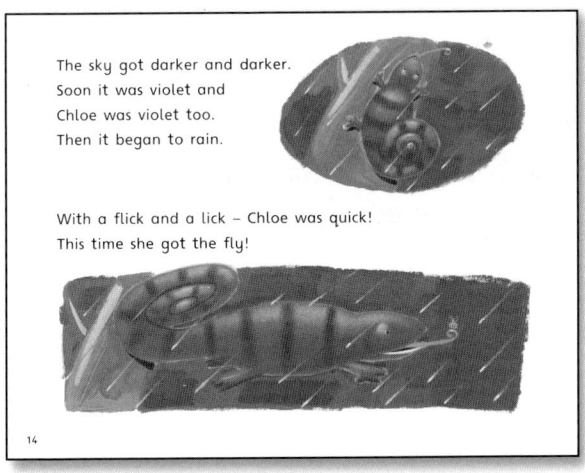

But Chloe slipped!
She fell
    down,
       down,
          down,
through the rainbow.

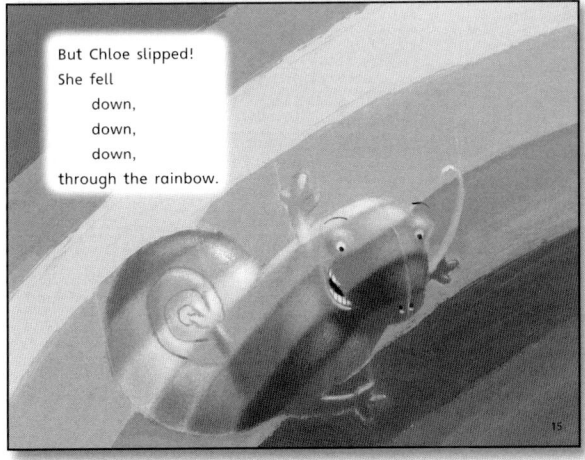

Chloe sat in the sun
and waited for another fly...

After Reading

Revisit and Respond

T Ask the children to re-read the story aloud, and discuss the rhyming words and rhythm in the story.

T Ask the children to name the colours Chloe turned in sequence. What do these colours make? (*a rainbow*)

T Ask them to think about where Chloe might go next to chase a fly. Where would she go and what colour would she turn? Take it in turns round the group to make up a story.

S Using words that rhyme with 'ick', ask the children to make up some silly sentences (e.g. *Mick was quick to kick the brick to the thick stick*).

S Ask the children to look at the way 'down' is written on page 15. Ask them to think of interesting ways to write other words (e.g. *up, up, up; round, round, round; left, right, left, right;* etc). Ask them to write their ideas on whiteboards.

W Ask them to make a list of all the 'ed' words in the story. Ask them to generate more words that end in 'ed' and add to list on teacher's whiteboard.

W Ask them to look at the title 'Chloe the Chameleon' and make a list of other words that have 'ch' making a 'k' sound. (E.g. *chaos, character, ache, chemist, stomach, Christopher, chorus*).

Follow-up

Independent Group Activity Work

This book is accompanied by two photocopy masters, one with a reading focus, and one with a writing focus, which support the main teaching objectives of this book. The photocopy masters can be found in the Planning and Assessment Guide.

PCM 11 (*reading*)

PCM 12 (*writing*)

Writing

Guided writing: Write the story from the point of view of the fly.

Extended writing: Write another Chloe story, using new places for her to go, and new colours for her to turn.

Assessment Points

Assess that the children have learnt the main teaching points of the book by checking that they can:

- identify patterns of rhyme and rhythm in rhyming text
- identify and generate words that rhyme with 'quick'
- use word ending 'ed' for past tense to support reading and writing.